For Ella – KU
For all my nephews and nieces – AC

The Sophie Rabbit Books:
Sophie and Abigail
Sophie and the wonderful picture
Sophie and the Mother's Day card
Sophie in charge

SOPHIE AND THE MOTHER'S DAY CARD
First published in North America by Good Books (2005), Intercourse, PA 17534
International Standard Book Number: 1-56148-481-4 (paperback edition)
International Standard Book Number: 1-56148-479-2 (hardcover edition)

Text copyright © Kaye Umansky 1993
Illustrations copyright © Anna Currey 1993
First published in Great Britain in Gollancz Children's Paperbacks 1995
by Victor Gollancz, a division of the Cassell group.
Produced by Mathew Price, Ltd., Dorset, England.

Printed in China

Kaye Umansky
Sophie and the Mother's Day card

Illustrated by Anna Currey

Good Books

Intercourse, PA 17534
800/762-7171
www.goodbks.com

It was coming up on Mother's Day, and everyone in Mrs. Badger's class had made a special card.

Sophie Rabbit was very proud of hers. It had a daffodil stuck on the front made of yellow paper and an egg carton. There were butterflies and flowers around the border. Inside, in her best writing, she had put:

To Mom with lots of love from Sophie.

It had taken her ages.

"That's a good daffodil," said Trevor
Otter, the new boy. Sophie didn't know
him yet. He was rather big and rather noisy.
"I can't do daffodils," said Trevor.

Sophie looked. It was true. Trevor's
card was a complete mess.

"I'm good at being an airplane,
though," said Trevor, zooming off.

At quiet time, Sophie ran to get her card – and got a nasty shock. The card was there all right, but where was the daffodil?

Someone had torn it off! What a mess it looked now. Poor Sophie. Two big ears spilled over onto her whiskers.

"Oh dear! Whatever could have
happened?" cried Mrs. Badger when
Sophie showed her the ruined card.
"What a shame, Sophie. It was such
a lovely card, too."

Out by the gate, Sophie's dad was waiting to walk her home.

"Bad day, Soph?" he asked.

"Awful," sighed Sophie. "Someone ripped the daffodil off Mom's card – look. I've got nothing to give her now."

"Oh dear." George Rabbit looked grave. "That is a pity. Can't you make another one?"

"No time. And I don't have the right things."

"Hmm. Tell you what. We'll take the long way home, shall we? You never know – the walk might cheer you up."

The long way home lay through the woods. Birds sang and spring breezes rustled around them, but Sophie couldn't stop thinking about the spoiled Mother's Day card.

George Rabbit stopped by a mossy bank.

"Look, Soph. Primroses. Did you know they're Mom's favorite flowers? I think I might have an idea about that card of yours ...."

Mother's Day dawned warm and sunny. For once, baby Gareth slept late, so Mrs. Rabbit had breakfast in bed for a treat. She was sipping her carrot juice when Sam and Louise came running in with their presents.

"It's a picnic basket," explained
Louise, jumping on the bed. "I wove it.
It's got a special place for salad
dressing."

"Amazing!" said Mrs. Rabbit.

"And I made you this clay pot,"
said Sam proudly. "For flowers."

"Beautiful!" marveled Mrs. Rabbit.

Then it was Sophie's turn. She
stepped forward and held out a tiny
bunch of pale yellow primroses.

The pretty homemade gift tag said:

To Mom with lots of love from Sophie.

"Oh, Sophie!" said Mrs. Rabbit. "The first primroses of spring! How did you know I like primroses best of all?"

"As much as daffodils?" asked Sophie anxiously.

"More," said Mrs. Rabbit, giving her a huge hug.

The rest of the day was perfect. They
packed Louise's hamper with lettuce
rolls and carrot cake and had a picnic
on the hill.

In a place of honor were Sophie's primroses in Sam's pot, which only leaked slightly. After tea they played games. Gareth fell in some stinging nettles and nearly cried — but didn't.

Mrs. Rabbit said it was the best Mother's Day ever. Sophie forgot about her ruined card — until the next day.

The next day was school. Mrs. Rabbit and Mrs. Otter were chatting on the playground. "Did you enjoy Mother's Day?" asked Mrs. Rabbit.

"I certainly did," said Mrs. Otter. "My Trevor made me a card with a lovely daffodil on it. It must have taken him ages. I was so pleased. He's usually only interested in airplanes."

Sophie looked at Trevor Otter.

Trevor looked ashamed.

"I'd like a word with you, Trevor," said Sophie.

"Well?" said Sophie when they were out of earshot. "What have you got to say for yourself?"

Trevor couldn't meet her angry eyes. He hung his head.

"I'm sorry," he muttered miserably.

"I know I shouldn't have done it. I just wanted to please my mom. You won't tell, will you?"

Sophie looked at him. For some reason, he didn't look as big as usual.

"No," said Sophie. "I won't tell."

Just then the bell rang.

"Come on," said Sophie, grasping
him firmly by the paw. "You're sitting
by me this morning. I'm going to help
you make a daffodil so you won't
need to take mine next time."

"Really? Thanks," said Trevor
humbly, adding hopefully:

"Do you think, if there's time, we
could make a paper airplane, too?"

"Both," smiled Sophie. "We'll
make both."

And that's exactly what they did.